D0258069

For Sally

This book has been assessed as Stage 8
according to *Individualised Reading*, by
Bernice and Cliff Moon, published by
The Centre for the Teaching of Reading,
University of Reading
School of Education.

First published 1987 by Walker Books Ltd
87 Vauxhall Walk, London SE11 5HJ

This edition published 1989

Printed in Italy by Grafedit S.p.A.

British Library Cataloguing in Publication Data
Hawkins, Colin and Jacqui
The wizard's cat.
I. Title
823'.914[J] PZ7
ISBN 0-7445-1389-8

THE WIZARD'S CAT

Written and illustrated by
Colin and Jacqui Hawkins

WALKER BOOKS
LONDON

Hello cat.

I wish I wasn't a cat.
I'm tired of that.

Who would you like to be?

Like to be? Someone better than me!

Al-a-kazam! Al-a-kazee!
Be a sailor on the sea!

No! No! The sea's too rough for me!

Fiddle-de-dee! Now you shall be a monkey up a tree!

No! No!
The tree's too high
for me!

Grumble, rumble, fo-fum-fee!
What about a bumble bee!

No! No!
I don't want hairy
knees and flowers
make me sneeze!

Hippity hoppity skippity roo!
Be a rabbit, that's best
for you!

No! I don't think it's funny being a bunny!

Then Split! Splat! Be a wizard's cat!

Yes,
I like
that!

Happy now?

Yes, now I can see it's best to be me!

MORE WALKER PAPERBACKS

THE PRE-SCHOOL YEARS

John Satchwell & Katy Sleight

Monster Maths

ODD ONE OUT   BIG AND LITTLE
COUNTING   SHAPES   ADD ONE   SORTING
WHAT TIME IS IT?   TAKE AWAY ONE

FOR THE VERY YOUNG

John Burningham

Concept books

COLOURS   ALPHABET
OPPOSITES   NUMBERS

Byron Barton

TRAINS   TRUCKS   BOATS   AEROPLANES

PICTURE BOOKS

For All Ages

Colin McNaughton

THERE'S AN AWFUL LOT OF WEIRDOS IN OUR NEIGHBOURHOOD
SANTA CLAUS IS SUPERMAN

Russell Hoban & Colin McNaughton

The Hungry Three

THEY CAME FROM AARGH!
THE GREAT FRUIT GUM ROBBERY

Jill Murphy

FIVE MINUTES' PEACE
ALL IN ONE PIECE

Bob Graham

THE RED WOOLLEN BLANKET
HAS ANYONE HERE SEEN WILLIAM?

Philippa Pearce & John Lawrence

EMILY'S OWN ELEPHANT

David Lloyd & Charlotte Voake

THE RIDICULOUS STORY OF GAMMER GURTON'S NEEDLE

Nicola Bayley

Copycats

SPIDER CAT   PARROT CAT   CRAB CAT
POLAR BEAR CAT   ELEPHANT CAT

Peter Dallas-Smith & Peter Cross

TROUBLE FOR TRUMPETS

Philippe Dupasquier

THE GREAT ESCAPE

Sally Scott

THE THREE WONDERFUL BEGGARS

Bamber Gascoigne & Joseph Wright

AMAZING FACTS BOOKS 1 & 2

Martin Handford

WHERE'S WALLY?
WHERE'S WALLY NOW?